jRA

discovering GRAPH

secrets

Experiments, puzzles, and games exploring graphs

discovering GRAPH secrets

Sandra Markle

Experiments, puzzles, and games exploring graphs

ATHENEUM BOOKS FOR YOUNG READERS

For Rachel, Katy, and Kyle, who show everyone how much fun it can be to discover graph secrets.

The author would like to thank the following for sharing their enthusiasm and expertise: Dr. Terry Wood, Purdue University; Dr. Gerald H. Krockover, Professor, School Mathematics and Science Center, Purdue University; Dr. Clarence Dockweiler, Texas A&M University; Shirley M. Frye, Mathematics Education Consultant. Special thanks to Constance Parramore for her creative assistance!

Atheneum Books for Young Readers
An imprint of Simon & Schuster Children's Publishing Division
1230 Avenue of the Americas
New York, New York 10020

Book design by Patti Ratchford.
The text of this book is set in Horley Old Style.
Printed in the United States of America. First Edition.
10 9 8 7 6 5 4 3 2 1

Library of Congress Cataloging-in-Publication Data
Markle, Sandra.
Discovering graph secrets : experiments, puzzles, and games exploring graphs /
Sandra Markle.—1st ed.
p.   cm.
Includes index.
Summary: Contains activities dealing with charts and graphs, showing how to construct them, what can be plotted, and how they illustrate mathematical concepts.
ISBN 0-689-31942-8 (guaranteed reinforced binding)
1. Graphic methods—Juvenile literature. [1. Graphic methods.]
I. Title.
QA90.M27   1997
001.4'226—dc20   96-15435   CIP   AC

Photo credits: Rob McDonald, Atlanta: cover, i, 9, 12, 14, 15, 22, 33. National Park Service: 2. Cornell Laboratory of Ornithology: 6, 7. Brian Parsons: 19. Brookfield Zoo: 21. Peter Tyack, Woods Hole Oceanographic Institution: 26, 27. Graphs by William Markle, CompuART.

contents

GETTING STARTED

Look at the picture of Mount Rushmore in South Dakota. What if you wanted someone who had never seen this memorial to know what it looks like? Which is likely to be the easiest way to share this information—a written description or a photo? A picture is easiest, of course. A picture is also more likely to help the person understand the memorial's complex structure.

Graphs are like photos. They make it easy to present and analyze large amounts of numerical and factual information. There are four basic kinds of graphs for different approaches to processing and presenting data: bar graphs, pictographs, line graphs, and circle graphs.

Here are examples of the four kinds of graphs.

Bar graphs make it easy to compare things.

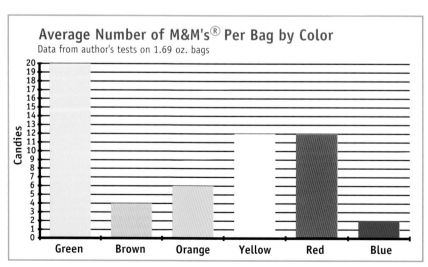

Pictographs

use pictures to convey ideas along with comparisons.

Favorite Sherbet Flavors
Fictional Data - Each Scoop = 5 People

Number of People

Blueberry Lime Orange Raspberry Strawberry Pineapple

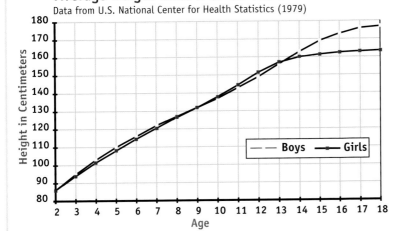

Average Height from 2 to 18 Years
Data from U.S. National Center for Health Statistics (1979)

Height in Centimeters

Age

— — Boys — ■ — Girls

Line graphs

show how something changes.

A circle graph,

which is often called a pie chart, makes it possible to see what part of a whole something is.

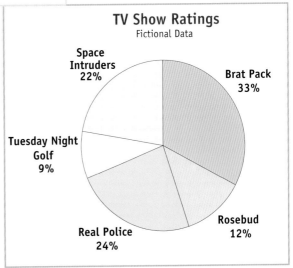

TV Show Ratings
Fictional Data

Space Intruders 22%

Brat Pack 33%

Tuesday Night Golf 9%

Rosebud 12%

Real Police 24%

3

A

graph reveals two kinds of information: the facts being considered and the results of a study or investigation. Those facts are organized into a list along either the horizontal or vertical side of the graph, on what are called the axes of the graph. The horizontal axis is called the x–axis; the vertical axis is called the y–axis. The results of the investigation are shown using a scale. In bar or line graphs, if the list of facts is along the x–axis, the scale is along the y–axis. Pictographs use symbols—each whole or part representing a specified amount of the data. A circle graph doesn't have axes. Instead, like a sliced pie, it is divided into wedges—one for each of the known facts. A circle graph makes it easy to compare related facts.

Now, be a detective and examine the sample graphs on pages 2 and 3.

① How many of the M&Ms in a ten–ounce bag were red? Were more M&Ms red or green?

② How many more people prefer orange sherbet to lime? Which is more popular—pineapple or raspberry sherbet?

③ How tall can you expect an average thirteen–year–old boy to be? A thirteen–year–old girl?

④ What percent of the viewing audience liked "Brat Pack" best? Which show was watched by the fewest people? (Clue: A percent is a fraction of 100. For example, 24 percent of this circle graph is 24/100 of the total imaginary viewing audience).

⑤ Describe some information you find in each graph.

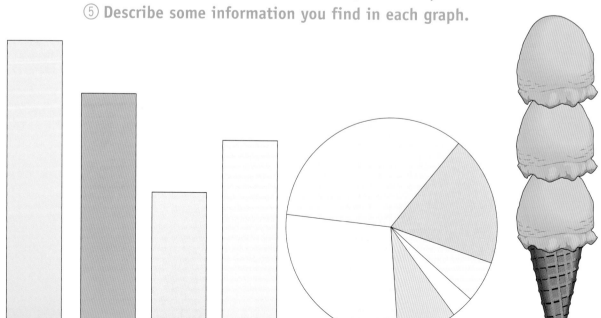

When the action in this book calls on you to construct your own graph, follow these steps:

1. Plan what you'll do to gather the information.

2. Decide how you'll organize the data you collect.

3. Select the appropriate scale for presenting the results. For example, look at the scale for M&Ms on page 2. What was the highest number on this scale? By how many M&Ms did the scale increase at each level? On the heights graph, how much did the scale change at each number to show average height increases among boys and girls? Why do you suppose the heights scale didn't start at zero centimeters?

4. Label the horizontal axis and the vertical axis if it's a bar or line graph. (There are special instructions on page 33 for constructing a circle graph.)

5. Record the results on your graph.

6. Give your graph a title that will let someone else understand what information it provides.

When you're ready for more action, read on. This book is packed with mysteries to solve and puzzles to figure out—all with the help of graphs. You'll also find out how people use graphs to solve real-life mysteries.

Cape May Warbler

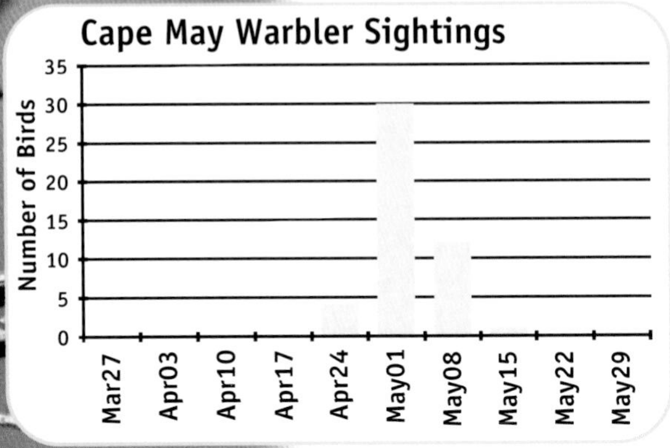
Cape May Warbler Sightings
Number of Birds
35
30
25
20
15
10
5
0
Mar27
Apr03
Apr10
Apr17
Apr24
May01
May08
May15
May22
May29

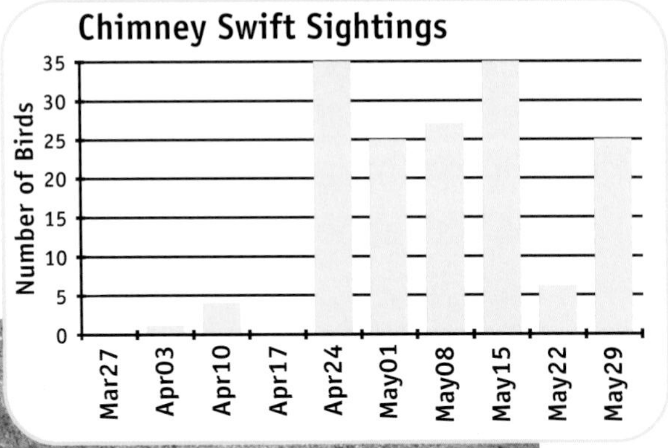
Chimney Swift Sightings
Number of Birds
35
30
25
20
15
10
5
0
Mar27
Apr03
Apr10
Apr17
Apr24
May01
May08
May15
May22
May29

American Goldfinch

Chimney Swift

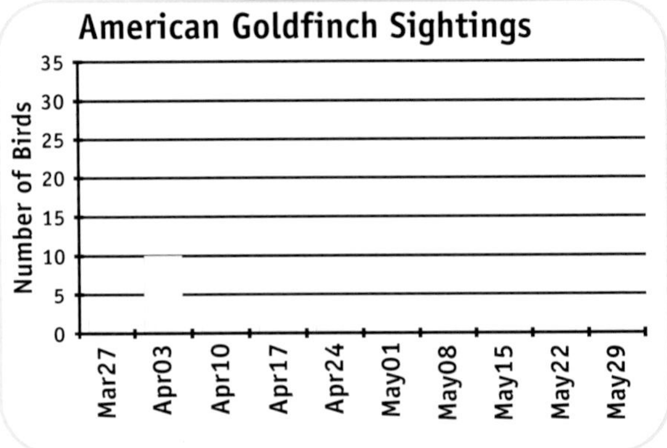
American Goldfinch Sightings
Number of Birds
35
30
25
20
15
10
5
0
Mar27
Apr03
Apr10
Apr17
Apr24
May01
May08
May15
May22
May29

The data for these graphs was provided by Georgann Schmalz, Ornithologist, Fernbank Science Center.

solving BAR GRAPH mysteries

Bar graphs let you quickly compare things. And in each of these mysteries, you'll find the most important clues are revealed in how the information stacks up. Ready for action? Then don't wait another minute to get started.

The Mysterious Visitor

Fernbank Forest, a protected sixty–four–acre forest in the heart of Atlanta, Georgia, is home to many different kinds of birds. On April 24, 1993, bird watchers in Fernbank Forest spotted chimney swifts, Cape May warblers, northern cardinals, and American goldfinches. Only one of these kinds of birds lives in the forest year-round. Another was a winter resident about to head north. Still another kind was a summer resident who had just arrived. The remaining bird was a tourist just passing through. Can you identify the bird that was the tourist?

The graphs next to the birds will help. These show how many of each kind were spotted over a period of ten weeks from March 27 through May 29. Analyze these graphs. As you work, write a step–by–step list of what you discover and the strategy you used to come to a conclusion.

When you think you can identify the visiting bird, put your strategy to work again. Now, can you figure out which kind of bird is the permanent resident? Check yourself on page 34.

Northern Cardinal

Northern Cardinal Sightings

Guess Who's Coming for Dinner?

Just like you, seed–eating birds have favorite foods. Look at the picture of the different kinds of seeds that are commonly put in a bird feeder. What kinds of seeds do you think are the most popular with birds in your area? You may not be able to get all of these kinds of seeds, but you should be able to get at least three different kinds. Some birds won't pick up seeds from the ground and will only feed at hanging or platform feeders. But you can then follow these steps to test what your local ground–feeding birds like best:

① Take down any feeders that might draw birds away from your test and keep them down during the entire investigation.

② Put out piles of three different kinds of seeds. Keep the piles completely separate from each other.

③ Watch in the morning and again in the afternoon. As soon as you see birds coming to feed, start timing. Observe for at least fifteen minutes, recording the kind of seed each visiting bird eats. If a bird eats more than one kind of seed, record that also.

④ Between observations, add more seeds to the piles as needed so that the size of the pile doesn't affect the birds' feeding decision.

⑤ Squirrels may come to feed too. You can either record what kind of seed they prefer, or you can wait until they leave, then add more seed and start your observations over.

At the end of the week, use the sample bar graph to construct a graph. It should show along one axis the kinds of seed you put out and have a scale for the number of birds along the other axis. Then fill in columns to show the total number of birds that ate each kind of seed. Make up your own title for this graph.

Which kind of seed was the most popular? Do you think another kind of seed might attract even more birds? Or might putting out a different seed attract different birds? (Clue: You'll probably need to use a bird book to help you identify the birds that dine with you.)

Design a plan that will let you test these ideas. In what ways would a bar graph help you share what you discover?

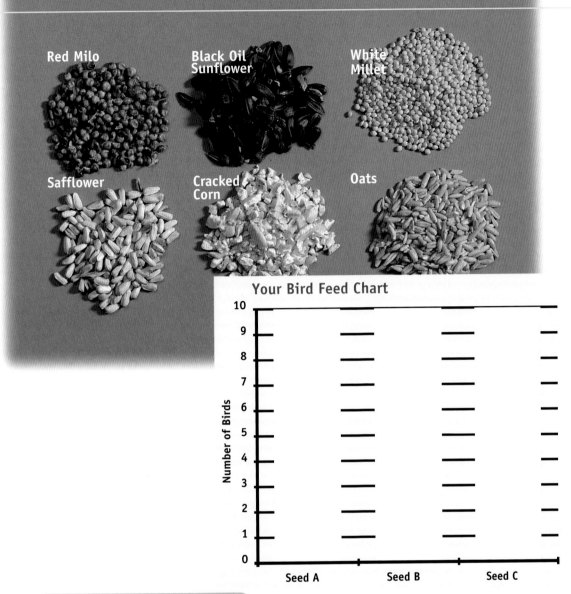

Red Milo

Black Oil Sunflower

White Millet

Safflower

Cracked Corn

Oats

Your Bird Feed Chart

Number of Birds

10
9
8
7
6
5
4
3
2
1
0

Seed A   Seed B   Seed C

Project Feeder Watch

If you live in North America and would like to participate in a continent-wide research study of what birds like to eat, join Project Feeder Watch. You can write or call for information at the headquarters in your country or organize your friends and conduct your own watch program.

Project Feeder Watch (United States)
Cornell Lab of Ornithology
159 Sapsucker Woods Road
Ithaca, New York 14850
(607–254–2414)

Project Feeder Watch (Canada)
Long Point Bird Observatory
Post Office Box 160
Port Rowan, Ontario N0E 1M0
Canada
(519-586-3531)

The Chocolate Chip Caper

There are a number of different brands of chocolate chip cookies on the market. If you're a real chocolate chip lover, like Max, you'll want to be sure you buy the brand that has the most chips per cookie. How can you help Max determine which brand to buy? A histogram will help. A histogram is a special kind of graph that shows a count of the number of times something occurs. In this case, the histogram shows the frequency of the number of chocolate chips found in each type of cookie. For example, it shows how many Chippies have only one chocolate chip per cookie, how many have two chocolate chips, and so forth. There is one histogram per brand of cookie. Comparing the histograms will let you easily see in which brand you are likely to consistently find a lot of chocolate chips in one cookie. Or the histogram may reveal that the number of chocolate chips per cookie varies greatly.

Compare the histograms. Which brand do you recommend that Max buy? How did the histogram help you make this choice? Check yourself on page 34.

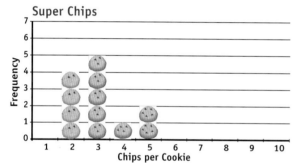

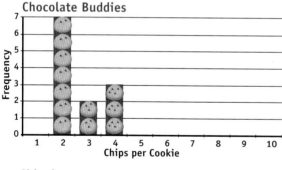

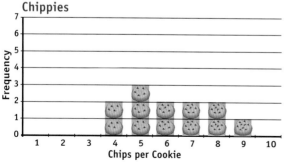

Extra Challenge: These aren't real brands of cookies. So which real brand has the most chips per cookie? First, choose three kinds to test. Next, randomly select ten of each brand. The best way to check for chips is to eat the cookies, so either complete your histograms over a number of days or have a party and invite your friends to help you munch.

Is it possible that more than one brand could be a good choice for chocolate chip lovers? Your histograms will tell you.

The Case of the Red-Hot Ruby

"Oh, Mr. Shovel. Thank heavens you're here." Sylvia Gotrocks raced across the ballroom to greet the detective.

"I hear somebody snatched your new necklace," Sam said.

"Cost me two million dollars," Oliver Gotrocks said. *"I hope you're as good as people say you are, Shovel."*

The ballroom was empty now, but earlier that evening there had been fifty guests celebrating Mrs. Gotrocks's birthday.

"Right after I opened the box with the ruby necklace, the lights went out," Mrs. Gotrocks reported.

"And a few seconds later, when the lights came on, the necklace was gone," Mr. Gotrocks said. *"I can't imagine how anyone could have taken it."*

"Well," Shovel said, *"my guess is that the crook is someone with very quick reflexes. If you can assemble everyone who was standing close to Mrs. Gotrocks when the lights went out, I know a test to check reflex actions that should help me identify the thief."*

You'll be better able to analyze the bar graph showing the results of Sam's test if you analyze this reflex action test yourself first. You'll need a ruler and at least four family members or friends to test. Make a copy of the sample graph, listing the names of your family and friends across the bottom. If you want to test your own reflexes, include your name too. Then follow the steps to give the reaction rate test.

① Hold the ruler vertically, gripping it at the top by the highest number.
② Have the person being tested hold the ruler vertically at the lowest number. Then have the person let go so his or her fingers are almost, but not quite, touching the ruler.

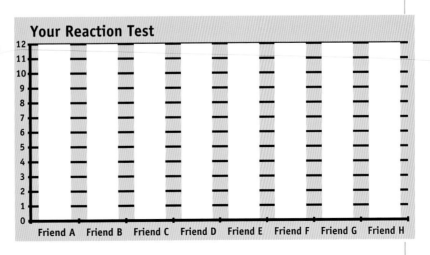

11

Tell the person to be ready to grab the ruler the instant it starts to drop.

③ Release the ruler without warning.

④ Check what number is closest to the person's thumb when he or she grabs the ruler. Color in a column on the graph up to that number.

⑤ If you are being tested, someone else will need to drop the ruler for you.

What do the numbers along the axis represent? What does a smaller number mean? Whose reaction was the fastest? How much difference was there between the fastest and the slowest reaction rates?

Now analyze the bar graph of the reaction rate test Sam gave to the suspects. Which of the suspects has the fastest reaction rate? When you think you know who the thief is, think how that person might have hidden the necklace. Check yourself on page 35.

Suspects' Reaction Tests
Fictional Data

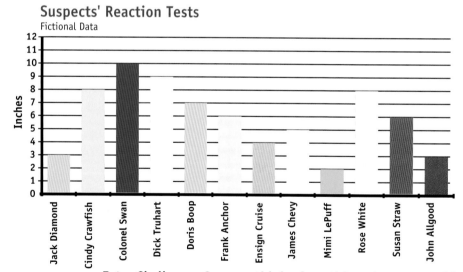

Extra Challenge: Can you think of anything else you could discover by testing people's reaction times? You'll probably think of other ideas, but here are two investigations to get you started: 1) Did girls or boys react faster? 2) Do people over thirty have a slower reaction time than people who are younger?

The more people you test, the more you can be sure your results show what's likely to occur every time. You should test at least twenty people (ten girls/ten boys; ten over thirty/ten under thirty).

Which Cereal Has the Most Iron?

You may be surprised to learn that some cereal makers actually add little flecks of iron to the cereal you eat. They do this because the human body needs a certain amount of iron to help it produce healthy red blood cells. Adding iron is a way to make cereals a better source of iron than they would be naturally. Not all cereals are fortified with the same amount of iron though. Which cereals do you think provide the most iron per one–ounce serving? Check the graph to find out.

Now, take a closer look at the graph to find out more about these cereals.

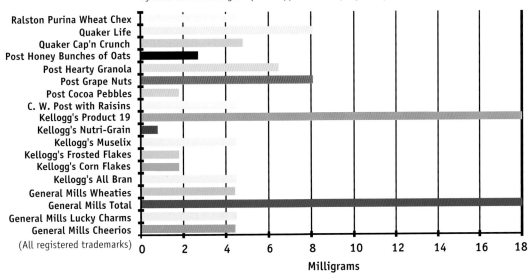

Milligrams of Iron Per One-Ounce Serving of Cereal

Data from Bowes & Church's Food Values of Portions Commonly Used by Jean A. T. Pennington (J. B. Lippincott Company 1994)

① Are there any cereals that have almost no iron?

② Which companies sell the cereals with the highest amount of iron per one-ounce serving?

③ Which of the cereals listed do you like to eat? (If you don't like any of them, just pick one at random.) If your bowl contains three ounces of cereal, how many milligrams of iron are you eating?

Here's another surprise. You can remove the iron from these cereals to take a closer look at what you're eating. To try this for yourself, you'll need a box of one of the

cereals that is an excellent source of iron. You'll also need a large self–sealing plastic bag, a small self–sealing plastic bag, and a strong bar magnet—one that can easily pick up at least a dozen steel paper clips. Or use three to four weaker bar magnets stacked together. Pour as much of the cereal as you possibly can into the large bag and seal the magnet inside the smaller bag. If the entire magnet will not fit inside the smaller bag, hold the bag tightly around the magnet and use only the covered part. Stir the magnet through the cereal several times.

Look closely. You should see some tiny dark bits stuck to the magnet. They will appear to be standing on end and if you move the magnet, they'll wiggle. Carefully pick a few off with your fingers. If you have a magnifying glass, use it for an even closer look. These are clusters of the little flecks of iron. Don't worry, the iron particles scattered through the cereal are too small to affect its taste or color. They're also tiny enough that they won't irritate your digestive tract.

When you're finished, sprinkle the cereal you used for your investigation outdoors for the birds to enjoy.

"O" My Goodness

How's your aim? How many O–shaped cereal loops can you toss into a bowl from 0.6 meters (2 feet)? How about from 1.2 meters (4 feet) or 1.8 meters (6 feet)? Take this challenge to find out how good your aim really is and make a bar graph to record the results. You'll need a box of O–shaped cereal, a cereal bowl, a measuring tape such as carpenters use, paper, and white glue. First, make a copy of the sample graph. Make it big enough so that you can actually use the glue to attach the cereal loops to your graph to record the results.

The tiny air pockets in this breakfast cereal act like life preservers, making the little Os float in milk.

When you're ready, place the cereal bowl on the table near the edge and measure a distance 0.6 meters (2 feet) away from the table. Stand at this distance and try to toss the cereal rings, one at a time, into the bowl. Glue the loops that land in the bowl one above the other to form a column on the graph. Next, measure 1.2 meters (4 feet) from the table and try again, gluing down your results. Repeat the test one more time from 1.8 meters (6 feet).

How much better did you do at 0.6 meters (2 feet) than at 1.8 meters (6 feet)? Can you do even better now that you've had practice? Try the series of tests a second time. Did your cereal–tossing skill improve?

Design your own test using the cereal loops and graph the results. Check if the cereal you tested is on the chart that shows its iron content. If it is, how much iron does a one–ounce serving contain?

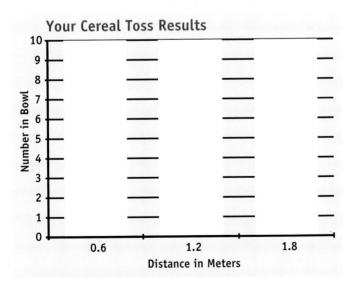

15

Who Has the Busiest Airport?

Every year millions of travelers pass through airports in cities in the United States and in other countries of the world. But which airports handle the most passengers each year? And how many millions annually pass through the busiest gateways?

This pictograph will let you find out. Remember, a pictograph uses symbols to represent numbers. In this pictograph of the world's ten busiest airports, each airplane represents ten million passengers.

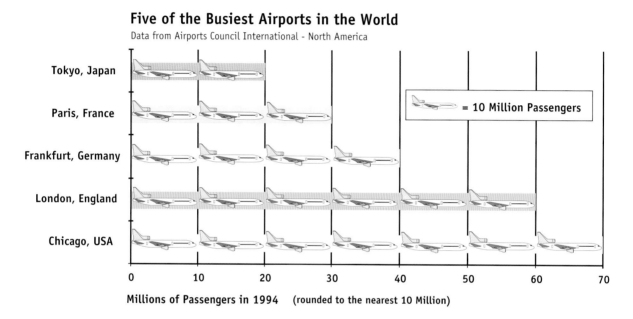

Five of the Busiest Airports in the World
Data from Airports Council International - North America

= 10 Million Passengers

Millions of Passengers in 1994   (rounded to the nearest 10 Million)

Now, using the pictograph, can you find out how many travelers passed through each of the top three busiest airports? How many more people passed through the busiest than the least busy airport? When you think you know, check yourself on page 35.

Extra Challenge: Now solve your own mini–mystery using a pictograph. How many pieces of each kind of trash does your family throw away or recycle in a week—glass, paper, plastic, metal, and other garbage? Decide what symbols you'll use to represent what's thrown out.

plotting with LINE GRAPHS

As you solve the first mystery in this section, you'll practice finding points on a line graph using graph coordinates, pairs of numbers that identify a specific point on a line graph. For example, in the graph below, look at the letter K in the lower right–hand corner. The coordinates for this letter are 9,1. The first number in the pair tells you how many lines to move along the x–axis, the horizontal axis. The second number tells you how many lines to move up the y–axis, the vertical axis. Try it yourself. Find the coordinates for the letter F in the upper right–hand corner of the graph. Then find the letter located by the coordinates 1,7.

Now, go on to investigate the mysteries in this section.

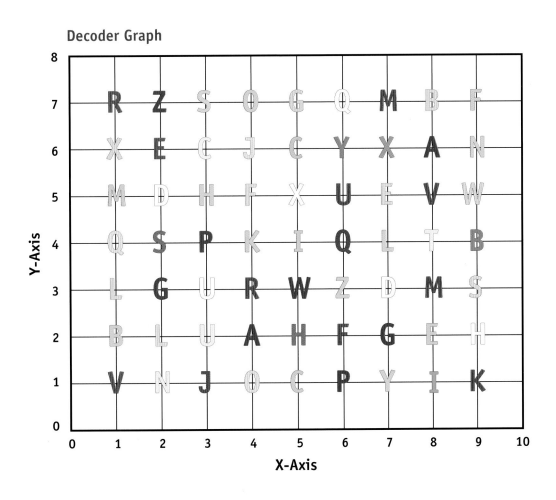

Decoder Graph

The Mystery Creature

I found a strange creature in the weeds at the edge of the pond. It was nearly 10 centimeters (4 inches) long. Its green body blended perfectly with the shape and color of the leaves. I watched it sitting there on its four big hind legs with its pair of tiny forelegs held close to its body. I wondered if it was watching me with its big eyes. Suddenly, the creature stretched out its tiny front legs and snatched an insect from the air.

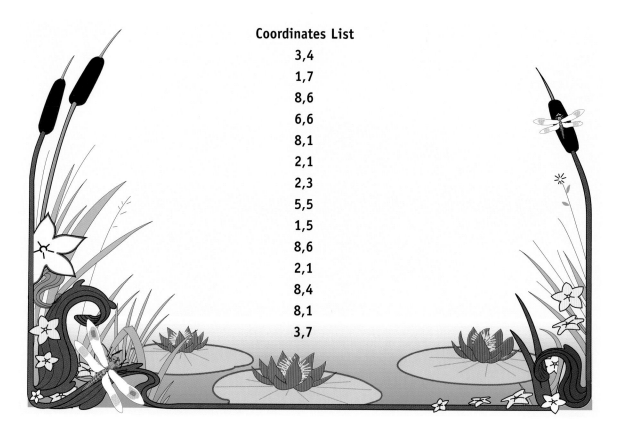

Coordinates List

3,4
1,7
8,6
6,6
8,1
2,1
2,3
5,5
1,5
8,6
2,1
8,4
8,1
3,7

Did you guess the identity of the mystery creature from this description? To check yourself, use the coordinates above to collect the letters from the decoder graph. Collect them in order to spell out the name of the creature. If you find an X on the graph, record it as a blank space. When you think you can name the creature, double–check yourself on page 35.

Hold a Roller Derby

Here's a fun activity with a mysterious twist. First, collect three empty plastic film cans with lids that push into the opening. If there aren't some around the house, you should be able to get these free at any store that handles film processing. You'll also need

books to stack up into a pile that is 2.5 centimeters (1 inch) high, then increases in stages to 5 centimeters (2 inches), 7.5 centimeters (3 inches), 10 centimeters (4 inches), 12.5 centimeters (5 inches), and 15 centimeters (6 inches) high. Use one thin flat book or a cutting board propped against this stack to create a ramp.

Set up the ramp on a smooth flat surface. Choose an area clear of obstacles. You'll need something such as pennies or dried beans to use as markers. Make a copy of the sample graph to record the results.

First, build the lowest tower and set the ramp in place. Use the film cans without the lids, rolling these one at a time down the center of the ramp. Place a marker where each can stops rolling. Even though the can may have rolled in a curve, measure straight from the bottom of the ramp to the marker. Do this for each of the three test cans. On scrap paper add together the three distances and divide by three to find the average distance the cans rolled. Make a dot on the graph to record the average distance the film cans rolled when the ramp was 2.5 centimeters (1 inch) high.

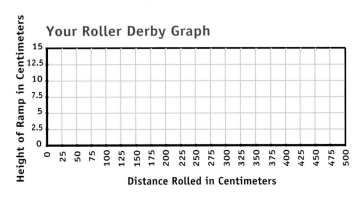

Your Roller Derby Graph

Height of Ramp in Centimeters (vertical axis: 0, 2.5, 5, 7.5, 10, 12.5, 15)

Distance Rolled in Centimeters (horizontal axis: 0, 25, 50, 75, 100, 125, 150, 175, 200, 225, 250, 275, 300, 325, 350, 375, 400, 425, 450, 475, 500)

Repeat, rolling the film cans down each of the higher ramps in turn. For each height, find the average distance the cans roll and record this on the graph.

Draw a line connecting the results of each set of tests. Then look for a pattern on the graphed results. In what way did the distance the cans rolled change as the ramp height increased? What do you think will happen if the ramp is inclined even more steeply? Test your prediction to find out if you're right.

Extra Challenge: Now, predict whether the cans will roll farther if they're filled with something, such as pennies or dried beans. Why do you think this will or will not happen? Test your prediction by setting up the ramp so it's 5 centimeters (2 inches) high. Fill the cans full of equal numbers of beans or pennies, snap on the lids, and let them roll. The results may surprise you! Check what you discovered with the solution on page 35.

Trouble at the Zoo

"I don't know what to do," Jane, the gorilla keeper, said. "Poor Gonzo loves bananas and he doesn't understand that I don't have any to give him."

"What are you talking about?" Ted, her assistant, asked. "I saw a whole case of bananas being unloaded this morning."

"Yes, but they're all green. I wish there was some way I could speed up how quickly the bananas ripen."

"Maybe there is," Ted said. "Let's experiment. Maybe we'll discover a way to make green bananas ripen faster."

First, Jane and Ted brainstormed, listing all the things they thought might work to change how quickly the bananas ripened. Next, they analyzed this list of ideas and chose the one they thought might be the most likely to work. Then they tested this idea.

You can conduct the test they tried. This suggestion came from Dr. Elizabeth A. Baldwin of the United States Department of Agriculture, Tropical Fruit Division. You'll need to make two copies of the sample graph to record your results—one for the control and one for the test. A control is set up identically to the test group but isn't changed during the test. Then anything that happens to the test group can be compared to the control. You'll need a dozen green bananas. Try to get undamaged fruits that are nearly identical in size.

First, label one graph "control" and one "test." Set aside six bananas to be the control, or fruit to which nothing is done. Seal the other six bananas in a paper bag. Punch a few tiny holes in the bag with a pencil point. (Dr. Baldwin said that a little air flow is needed to prevent bacteria growth.)

Check the total number of bananas in the control group that are ripe each day and record this on the graph by making an X with a red pencil. Also peek inside the bag and count how many of the test bananas are ripe. Record

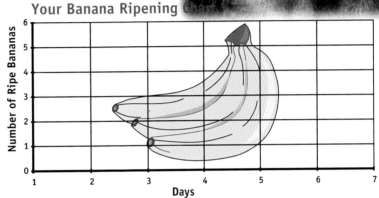

Your Banana Ripening C____

this on the graph using a blue pencil. When all six bananas are ripe, connect all the blue Xs with a blue line and all the red Xs with a red line. Only count the bananas as ripe when the peel is completely yellow. (Note: If the skin turns dark without turning yellow, the fruit has suffered damage.)

Did being inside a bag change how quickly the bananas ripened? Would this method help Gonzo get ripe bananas faster? If not, try the strategies in the Extra Challenge. Check the solution on page 35.

Extra Challenge: Now, test one or more other strategies. You can think up one of your own or try one of these experiment ideas suggested by Dr. Baldwin: put bananas in the refrigerator, coat with vegetable oil, or put bananas in a dark cupboard. Graph and analyze the results of your new test, seeing how the green bananas ripen over three to five days. Did one way work best? How do you know this?

What's in the Trunk?

"I can't get it open," Katy said after one last effort to pry open the latch with the screwdriver.

Rachel and Kyle had each had a turn trying to open the old trunk. Nothing worked. The friends stood side by side, staring curiously at the trunk they'd found in Kyle's attic. Kyle's mother thought it might have been in the house when they moved in, which made the trunk all the more mysterious.

They knew there was something inside. They had heard a soft thud when they tipped the old trunk up on one end.

"Look! There's a crack in the lid." Kyle pointed.

"It's too skinny to peek through," Katy complained.

Rachel said, "I've got an idea."

First, she used a piece of chalk to number every few centimeters alongside the crack. Then she drew a graph on a piece of paper. She also wrote these numbers along the bottom line of the graph. Next, she numbered up the side of the graph in ten–centimeter (4–inch) intervals.

After this, she put a tiny ball of clay on one end of a long string to help keep the string straight. Then she lowered the string through the crack in the trunk at the place she had chalked the number 1. When she felt the clay ball bump as though it had struck something, Rachel pinched the string where it touched the trunk lid. She pulled the string out and measured it to find out how much had been inside the trunk.

To record the distance from the crack to where the clay bumped something solid at point 1, Rachel went up from 1 on the x–axis to the level of the measurement. She made a dot at this point on the graph. Next, she continued checking the amount of string that could be lowered into the trunk before the ball touched something at each of the other numbers and recorded these measurements on the graph. Then she connected the set of points.

"Wow! Look at that," Kyle said.

"I think I can guess what's inside the trunk," Rachel said.

Either the hat, pumpkin, or boot is inside the trunk. To find out which is the mystery item, copy the graph below. Making the lines for the x–axis and the y–axis each 1.5 centimeters (0.6 inch) apart creates a graph that fits well on a sheet of paper. (You may choose to make the squares bigger or smaller.) Fill in the numbers on the x–axis and the y–axis as shown on the sample graph. Next, mark a dot at each of the points identified by the coordinates, drawing a line to connect these points as you go. Now, take a good look at the profile outlined on this line graph. Can you guess what's inside the old trunk? When you think you know, check yourself on page 35.

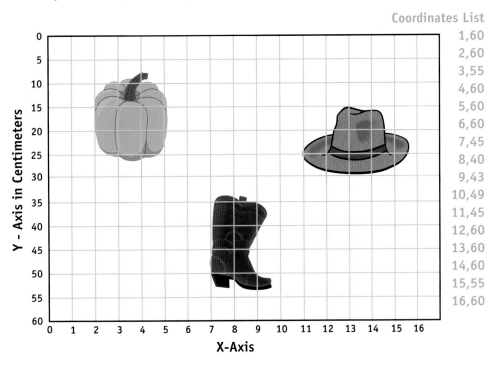

Coordinates List

1,60
2,60
3,55
4,60
5,60
6,60
7,45
8,40
9,43
10,49
11,45
12,60
13,60
14,60
15,55
16,60

Extra Challenge: Create this same kind of mystery for your friends to solve. First, cut a slit in a shoe box lid. Number from one through twenty along it. Hide something inside the box. Be sure to pick something with a simple profile, such as a shoe or even a soft drink can. If it's likely to slide around, anchor it with double-sided tape. Give your friends the following tools to work with: a graph, a ruler, and a string with a ball of clay at one end. Then tell them to use the string to measure the distance from the lid to the object inside at each point along the slit in your mystery box. Challenge them to create a line graph and use it to figure out what's inside the box.

Who Is the Message Bandit?

"What's up?" Sam Shovel asked, pushing his hat back from his face.

"It's the message bandit again," Detective Allen reported. "Ten burglaries in ten weeks—this time he broke into the mayor's house and stole a valuable painting."

"Must be smart to get past guards and a state–of–the–art security system. What clues did you find?"

"Nothing. This crook is clever."

"But there was a message on the answering machine?"

"Sure, like always." Detective Allen sighed. "And, like always, the voice was disguised. Won't do us any good. We've got four suspects—a security guard, the cook, a cleaning lady, and the gardener—who were recorded by the television monitors as being in the house at the time of the crime. We don't have any evidence, though, so we can't arrest anybody."

Sam Shovel said, "Give me the bandit's message and a tape recording of each suspect repeating that message. Then I'll tell you if one of your suspects is the bandit."

Help Sam Shovel figure out which of the suspects, if any, is the message bandit. This is a special type of graph called a spectrogram. This type of graph translates sounds into pictures by recording frequency, or high and low sounds. Sam Shovel was counting on the bandit producing the same pattern of sounds even when disguising his or her voice.

Based on the suspects' spectrograms on these pages, do you think one of the suspects could be the message bandit? What evidence from the graph helped you decide? Check your solution with Sam Shovel's on page 35.

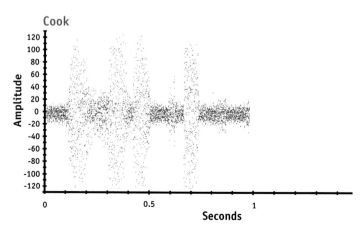

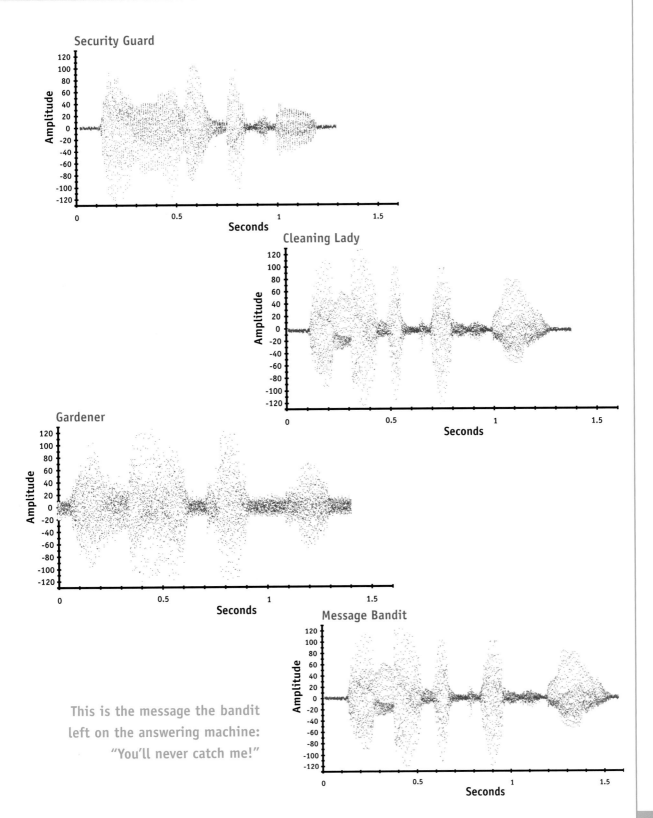

Security Guard

Cleaning Lady

Gardener

This is the message the bandit
left on the answering machine:
"You'll never catch me!"

Message Bandit

Is It a Boy or a Girl?

Here's a case of scientists using graphs in their research. Peter Tyack, who studied communications among bottle–nosed dolphins, recorded the whistles made by mothers and their calves. From these he generated the following spectrograms. Then, by studying these spectrograms, he learned that just as every person has a name, each bottle–nosed dolphin has a signature whistle, a set pattern of high and low sounds that the dolphin produces over and over. Dr. Tyack also discovered that male calves often have a signature whistle that is very similar to their mother's. Female calves usually produce a signature whistle that doesn't resemble their mother's.

Look at the spectrogram for Calf 1. Compare it to the spectrogram for Mother 1. Look for a pattern of high, low, rising, or descending frequencies similar to the mother's. Do you think Calf 1 is a male or a female? Now compare Calf 2's whistle to that of Mother 2. Do you think Calf 2 is a male or female? Why? Check your predictions on page 35.

The special light on each dolphin's head lights up when the animal makes a sound, so researchers can tell which of a group of dolphins is communicating.

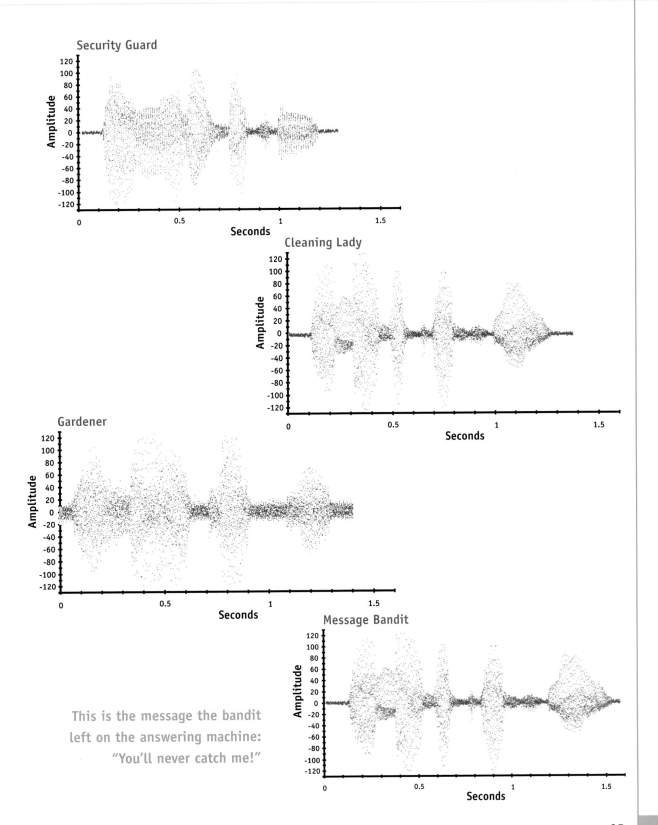

Security Guard

Cleaning Lady

Gardener

Message Bandit

This is the message the bandit
left on the answering machine:
"You'll never catch me!"

Is It a Boy or a Girl?

Here's a case of scientists using graphs in their research. Peter Tyack, who studied communications among bottle–nosed dolphins, recorded the whistles made by mothers and their calves. From these he generated the following spectrograms. Then, by studying these spectrograms, he learned that just as every person has a name, each bottle–nosed dolphin has a signature whistle, a set pattern of high and low sounds that the dolphin produces over and over. Dr. Tyack also discovered that male calves often have a signature whistle that is very similar to their mother's. Female calves usually produce a signature whistle that doesn't resemble their mother's.

Look at the spectrogram for Calf 1. Compare it to the spectrogram for Mother 1. Look for a pattern of high, low, rising, or descending frequencies similar to the mother's. Do you think Calf 1 is a male or a female? Now compare Calf 2's whistle to that of Mother 2. Do you think Calf 2 is a male or female? Why? Check your predictions on page 35.

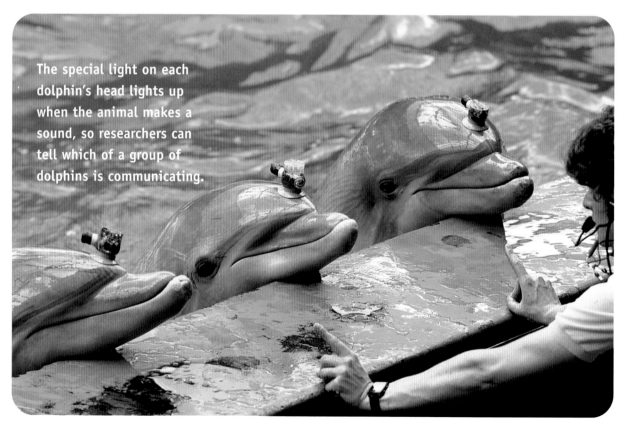

The special light on each dolphin's head lights up when the animal makes a sound, so researchers can tell which of a group of dolphins is communicating.

Mother #1's Whistle
Data from Dr. Peter L. Tyack/Woods Hole Oceanographic Institution

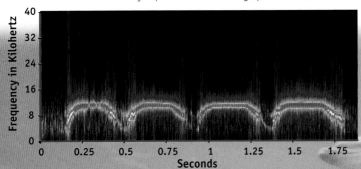

Whistles and clicks help mother and baby keep track of each other as they swim along.

Calf #1's Whistle
Data from Dr. Peter L. Tyack/Woods Hole Oceanographic Institution

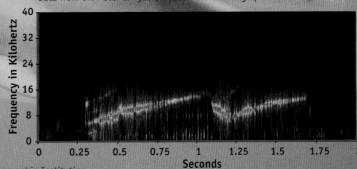

Mother #2's Whistle
Data from Dr. Peter L. Tyack/Woods Hole Oceanographic Institution

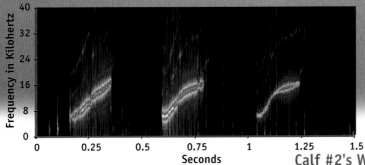

Calf #2's Whistle
Data from Dr. Peter L. Tyack/Woods Hole Oceanographic Institution

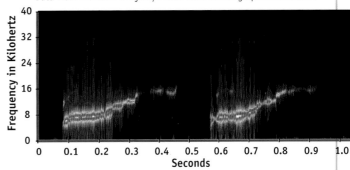

investigating CIRCLE GRAPHS

This time the mysteries you encounter can be solved when you see things in proportion. Circle graphs reveal how parts of something are related to the whole.

Project Garbage

Earlier you created a bar graph to learn what kinds of trash your family throws away. Now you'll be analyzing what kinds of trash cities usually dump in a landfill. This information was collected by Dr. W. L. Rathje's students at the University of Arizona as part of a program called the Garbage Project.

Just how much of the trash that ends up in a landfill is paper? Think how much of what you see thrown away at home and at school is paper. Ask your parents and other adults to estimate how much of what is thrown away at work is paper. Based on what you learn, guess how much of the total waste in a landfill is paper and then graph it. Draw a circle to represent everything that ends up in a landfill. Then think of this circle as a pie. Color in a pie–shaped wedge of the circle, like a slice of pie, that you think represents the portion that is paper.

Now decide how much of the trash that ends up in a landfill is made up of each of these other kinds of waste: glass, metal, plastic, garbage, and other stuff, such as old tires. Using different colors to represent the different kinds of trash, color and label a pie-shaped wedge for each one. Make bigger wedges for items you think represent most of the trash that's dumped. When you're finished, the entire landfill circle graph should be full.

Now compare your prediction to the circle graph showing what the Garbage Project discovered.

Extra Challenge: Take a paper grocery bag and squeeze it into as small a ball as you possibly can. Do the same thing to a plastic grocery bag. Which takes up more space in a landfill—paper or plastic grocery bags?

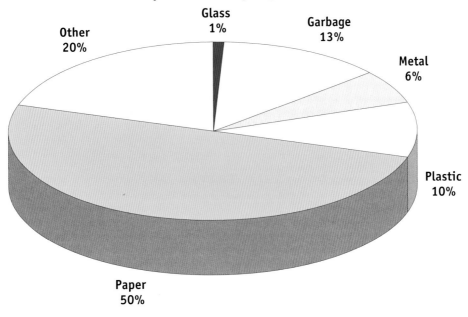

What's in a Landfill
Data from University of Arizona Garbage Project

Glass 1%

Garbage 13%

Metal 6%

Plastic 10%

Paper 50%

Other 20%

This graph was constructed based on the information collected by the Garbage Project. From 1987 to 1991, students dug into eleven different landfills at sites across the United States, sorting and analyzing trash. They were surprised by how little the garbage had changed after as long as twenty years in a landfill. Newspapers were still readable. Food items such as hot dogs and corn cobs were only slightly changed after five years.

Where Did It Go?

"Dad, I just can't live on my allowance," Samantha insisted. *"I've got to have a raise."*

"If you spent your money more wisely—" Dad began. But Samantha was ready for that argument.

"I don't waste my allowance," Samantha explained. *"Just take a look at the graphs I made to show how I spent my money during the last three weeks."*

Here are Samantha's graphs. What did Samantha spend the most on each week? The least? How much more did she spend on her mother than on her friend? Tell something else you learned about Samantha from these graphs.

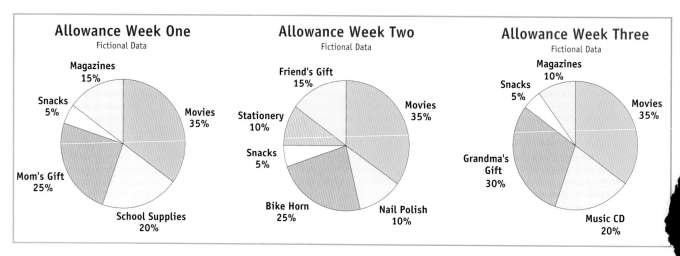

Allowance Week One
Fictional Data

- Magazines 15%
- Snacks 5%
- Movies 35%
- Mom's Gift 25%
- School Supplies 20%

Allowance Week Two
Fictional Data

- Friend's Gift 15%
- Stationery 10%
- Snacks 5%
- Bike Horn 25%
- Movies 35%
- Nail Polish 10%

Allowance Week Three
Fictional Data

- Magazines 10%
- Snacks 5%
- Movies 35%
- Grandma's Gift 30%
- Music CD 20%

Extra Challenge: Where does your allowance go? Keep careful records for one week. To figure out what percent of your money you spent on each item, divide the cost of that item into your total allowance. For example, if you get $5.00 and you spent $0.75 on snacks, divide $5.00 into $0.75. The answer is 15, which means that you spent 15 percent of your money on snacks. What percentage did you spend on entertainment? Other people? Other things?

Selling Zippy Soda

"Okay, we've got a problem," B. G. Thomas told his two assistants.

James Smathers was sweating. "W–what is it?"

"Fill us in, Boss," Clarisse Berk urged.

"Zippy Soda has asked our advertising agency to handle their new campaign. If they like our idea, they'll spend zillions on it."

Smathers smiled. "Sounds great to me, Boss."

"But Zippy Soda will only sign with us if we come up with an advertisement that reaches a lot of people and convinces them to buy Zippy Soda," Thomas announced.

Smathers groaned. "How can we figure out in advance what people will like and what they will remember?"

Clarisse had been scribbling wildly on her notepad. At last, she looked up and smiled. "If

I can tell you what kind of advertising campaign will be successful, will you give me a raise?"

"If you can tell me the best way to get the public interested in Zippy Soda, I'll double your salary," Thomas said.

Can Clarisse really deliver a successful advertising campaign? Here's the plan she wrote down:

① Make a list of the main types of media used for advertising.
② Make a list of the different styles of advertisements.
③ Select one hundred people at random.
④ Check that the people selected represent the entire soda-drinking population.
⑤ Survey this group about the kind of media they encounter most often. Find out which style of commercial they enjoy most.
⑥ Analyze these surveys. Figure out the trend.

Below are graphs showing what Clarisse learned when she made her list and surveyed a random sample of one hundred soda drinkers. Based on her results, what media will she recommend for the Zippy Soda advertising campaign? What style of advertisement will she suggest? When you think you know, check yourself on page 35.

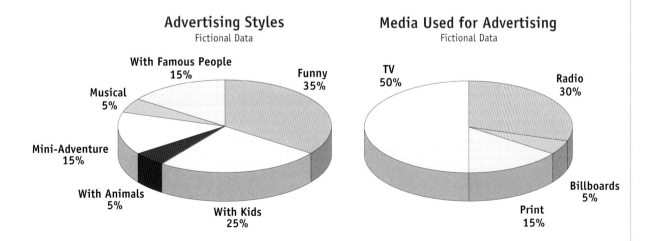

Fast Facts About Polling

Wonder how you can successfully conduct a survey or poll on your own? Here are some hints from Jack Ludwig, chief methodologist for The Gallup Organization, Inc., world famous for its surveys of public opinion:

① If you are only surveying part of a group, be sure your sample represents the larger group. For example, when checking audience reaction to movies, The Gallup Organization is careful to survey males and females equally. It also makes sure that it checks people of different ages and educational backgrounds and people from different parts of the country.

② Make the survey group as large as possible. The larger the sample, the more likely it is that this group will reflect the population it's supposed to represent.

③ Phrase questions carefully to make sure they don't reflect your own opinion and lead people to say the answer you want to hear.

What if you were going to conduct a poll in all of the world's countries? How would you reach people in countries where most homes don't have telephones? How would you get the data assembled from all the different countries in a way that would let you report the results in a timely fashion? Brainstorm. Make a list of all the possible problems. Then look over your list and imagine ways to deal with each of these problems. You may want to visit the library and read about communication systems used to reach remote areas. You may want to invent a new communication system that would make this project possible. In that case, draw a diagram of your idea and write a short description of how it works.

A Survey of Your Own

Now it's your turn. Surveys are a great way to check up on all sorts of things, including people's opinions and habits. For example, you might take a survey to get a sense of what people feel by asking one of these questions:

① What kind of pet do you like best: fish, dogs, cats, birds, other?

② What do you do for exercise: play a sport, walk, bicycle, swim, other?

③ With whom are you most comfortable discussing a problem: a family member, a friend, a teacher, a police officer, a doctor, other?

Or think of a survey question of your own. Next, select your survey group. Remember, for best results you should try to talk to one hundred people. And those people should be chosen at random to include a mix of men and women or boys and girls

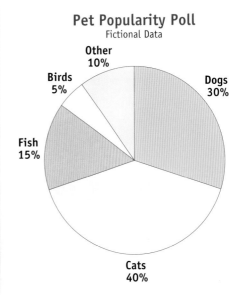

Pet Popularity Poll
Fictional Data

Other 10%

Birds 5%

Dogs 30%

Fish 15%

Cats 40%

of different ages and backgrounds. Of course, it isn't always possible to survey such a large group of people, but to make it easier to graph the results, survey an even number, such as ten, twenty, thirty, and so forth.

After you conduct your survey, sort the responses by the categories. For example, for the pet survey, you'd count up the total number of people who like fish best, the total number that like dogs best, and so forth.

Now, you're ready to construct a circle graph of the results. You'll need a compass and a protractor. A protractor is like a half circle. Its curved edge shows 180 equal parts, called degrees—half of the 360 degrees of a whole circle. First, use a compass to draw a circle. Then, mark the center of the circle with a dot and draw a straight line from that dot to any point on the circle. If you were to draw all the lines you could and still divide the circle into equal parts, you would be able to divide the circle into 360 equal parts; each of these parts is called a degree.

Next, divide the total number of people you surveyed into 360. Multiply that number by the number of people in each of your groups. For example, if you surveyed 100 people—100 divided into 360 equals 3.6 degrees per person. Twenty people like fish best, so 20 times 3.6 equals 72. This number can now be used to determine how much of the circle graph will represent this group. Place the 0 mark on the protractor where the first line you drew touches the circle. Then measure over as many degrees as your total—in this case 72 degrees. Make a mark and draw a line from the center of the circle to this point on the edge of the circle. Label this part of the circle "Fish" and color it bright blue. Now, multiply the number of dog lovers times 3.6. Place the protractor's 0 on the point where the new line you drew meets the circle. Then measure over the new number of degrees, mark this point, and draw another line from the center to the edge of the circle. Keep going until the circle graph is complete.

The End—Never!

Now you've discovered that graphs are fun and are useful tools for presenting and analyzing data. What's more, you've learned that graphs can help you tackle problems and make decisions. So even though this is the end of the book, there's lots of action ahead. Be curious and it won't be long before you're using graphs to discover more secrets. You'll also find lots of ways to use graphs to present the results of your own investigations. In fact, here are some more questions to get you started investigating:

① What is the most common bedtime for kids your age?

② How does the length of your shadow change from sunrise to sunset? Is there a pattern to the way it changes?

③ Does the surface it's on affect how long a top will spin?

④ Which of these sports is the most popular: soccer, baseball, volleyball, tennis, or basketball?

Solutions

P. 6 & 7: The Mysterious Visitor—Solution

The Cape May warbler is the mystery visitor. This kind of bird stops by the Fernbank Forest on its way to Maine. You probably figured this out by observing that there were none spotted until April, a lot observed early in May, and then none sighted after May 15. The northern cardinal is the permanent resident. The graph revealed about the same number of these birds sighted each week.

By analyzing the graphs, you also discovered that the American goldfinch is a winter resident and then leaves. In case you're wondering, the American goldfinch heads out of town to nest in open fields. The chimney swift is a summer resident. If you look up this kind of bird in a bird book, you'll find that it winters in the Caribbean. The numbers of this kind of bird sighted increased each week as more chimney swifts moved into the forest.

P. 10: The Chocolate Chip Caper—Solution

Max will be happiest with Chippies. Most of these cookies had lots of chips.

P. 11: The Case of the Red-Hot Ruby—Solution

The test revealed that Mimi LePuff, the maid, had the fastest reaction rate. When Sam Shovel pointed to Mimi, she admitted the theft. She had slipped the necklace into a glass of red punch.

P. 16: Who Has the Busiest Airport?—Solution

The three busiest airports are Chicago, Illinois, 70 million; London, England, 60 million; and Frankfurt, Germany, 40 million. Fifty million more people passed through the Chicago airport than the Tokyo airport.

P. 18: The Mystery Creature—Solution

If you had not already figured it out from the clues, you should have collected the letters to spell out "praying mantis." Although many people call them "preying" mantises, expert Lawrence E. Hurd of Washington and Lee University points out that "praying" is the correct word. These insects were originally named because their small front legs made them appear to be praying.

P. 19: Hold a Roller Derby—Solution

You should have discovered that the distance the empty cans rolled increased as the height of the ramp increased. However, the full cans did not travel nearly as far. Dr. Ralph Buice of the Fernbank Science Center (Atlanta, Georgia) explained that this is the result of the forward and backward motion of the beans or pennies inside the cans. Even if you packed in as many beans or pennies as you could, these objects would still be able to move a little. As these objects moved, they used up energy that otherwise could have propelled the can forward.

P. 20: Trouble at the Zoo—Solution

Sealing the bananas inside the bag should have caused them to ripen faster. Fruit just naturally gives off small amounts of a chemical called ethylene as it ripens. Being inside a bag traps any ethylene gas that's given off. Increasing the amount of exposure bananas have to this gas speeds up the ripening process. If Gonzo's lucky, most of the bananas in the bag will ripen overnight.

P. 22: What's in the Trunk?—Solution

The hat is inside the trunk.

P. 24: Who Is the Message Bandit?—Solution

Based on comparing the speech patterns, Sam announced that the message bandit was the cleaning lady. After making the arrest, Detective Allen discovered that the cleaning lady wasn't a "lady" at all. The message bandit was an out-of-work actor named Willy McGee.

P. 26: Is It a Boy or a Girl?—Solution

Calf 1 is a female. Calf 2 is a male. Did you see the ways in which Calf 2's signature whistle is like its mother's?

P. 29: Where Did It Go?—Solution

Samantha spent the most on going to the movies. She spent the least on snacks. She spent 10 percent more on her mother than on her friend. You might tell any number of things about Samantha from these graphs. For example, you can tell she has a bicycle and likes to wear nail polish.

P. 30: Selling Zippy Soda—Solution

After analyzing the data revealed on the circle graphs, Clarisse suggested that Zippy Soda use a funny television commercial for their new advertising campaign.

Index